About the Comic

Predators of Denali started development in early 2017 and finished in late 2023...6 years! I did a lot of other work in-between pages, so it makes sense that it would take so long.

While Denali and a few other details exist, this is a fictional earth. Inspired by Native Alaskan cultures, but not directly copied. The names, markings, clothing and more are either ficticious, or picked by me for this fantasy setting. The only exception is the language used on some of the pages, which is Koyukon Athabascan. I believe sharing real-life elements like endangered languages make the story more memorable and grounded by the audience, even if it is 'just' an adult furry comic.

I practiced balancing story with sex in this comic, and have grown to love all of the characters. After many revisions, I can finally say the same about the story. So I hope you will enjoy it too!

TALA...
...TALA...
WAKE UP!

BWAH!
HEY, WOAH! CALM DOWN PUP!
HAH
HA
HAH
HAHH...
H-HUH?
YOU WERE OUT COLD! WE ALMOST REACHED THE LAKE BEFORE WE NOTICED YOU GONE.
YOU ALL RIGHT?
HUFF
Y..YEAH..
SIGH~
WE MAY BE FAR AWAY FROM THE DANGERS OF THE FERAL LANDS, BUT SLEEPING OUT IN THE OPEN ISN'T A GOOD HABIT--
ESPECIALLY MIDDAY!
BRUSH
I KNOW, A'LE. I JUST...
GET THAT WEAK DOG UP!
WE'RE LATE, NO THANKS TO HER.
RUB
RUB
IGNORE KIGA...
YOU READY?
RRRRGH...
YEAH, YEAH.
SNIFFLE

PREDATORS
OF DENALI
ALMOST THERE...

I'M THE ONLY ONE OF AGE THIS SEASON...
CHATTER
DON'T WORRY,
THE URSA TRIBE IS SENDING ONE OF THEIR OWN WITH YOU.
WE'VE ALL TAKEN THE LONG CLIMB BEFORE. YOU'LL BE FINE!
ALRIGHT...

CHIEF ASKA!
LATE WOLVES ARE RARE! ENAA NEENYO!*
THIS MUST BE THE NEW YOUNG HUNTRESS! ADULT AND STRONG!
hehe
YOU'RE TOO KIND, ASKA; I'M JUST A TWIG OF A WOLF.
YOU UNDERSELL YOURSELF, LADY WOLF! WHAT NEWS HAVE YOU?

WELL, WE HEARD--

DAALEK!*
*=SHUT UP!
IT'S YOUR CLIMB, BUT YOU DO NOT SPEAK FOR US! ARE YOU A DIPLOMAT?!
SNRL
N...NO, KIGA--
CHOOSE WORDS WISELY, REMEMBER YOUR PLACE, AND WHEN TO SPEAK!
HUFF...
YES, SIR.
N-NO NEED TO YELL, KIGA!
NEWS FROM THE TACOMA AVIANS IS THAT PREDATORS ACROSS THE WORLD ARE BEHAVING...'ODDLY'.
ATTACKING AND...MATING... WITH BIPEDAL PREY.
I HATE TO SAY IT, BUT WE TOO IN THE TELIDA PACK HAVE BEGUN TO FEEL THIS URGE TO HUNT ALL PREY,
AND SINCE WE GUARD THE BORDER OF DENALI'S SENTIENT RANGE...
WELL...
OUR HERITAGE AS PROTECTORS WOULD BE THREATENED.

NGH
WELL NOW,
I CAN SEE YOUR PREDICAMENT. YOU WOULDN'T WANT THE -
HUFF
HNNNGH..
AHEM...
EXCUSE ME.
HM
KOFF...
MHH-
...SENTIENT DENALI PREY TRIBES TO FEEL UNEASY.
HUFF

CORRECT.
FERAL PREY IS BECOMING HARDER TO FIND. WE'VE TRIED TO SUPPLEMENT WITH INSECTS, FISH, AND SOME FLORA...
BUT THIS URGE TO HUNT GROWS, AND THESE STAND-INS WILL NOT LAST.
I-I SEE...
NGH
--WELL! WE CAN ASK THE SHEEP, ELK, HARES...
HFF..
HMM...
HMM.. IS ASKA SICK?

AS WE ALL KNOW, THE LANDS CLOSEST TO THE MOUNTAIN IS WHERE WE WALK UPRIGHT, THINK, AND SPEAK AS WE DO.
BEYOND THAT, FERAL PREDATORS AND PREY RULE THE LANDS...
WE'VE ONLY EVER HUNTED FERAL PREY, BUT AS WE VENTURE FURTHER OUT, THIS URGE TO HUNT TAKES GREATER HOLD.
SNRT
HNNN...

WELL...THE SACRED STONES ON THE WORLD'S MOUNTAIN PEAKS ARE WHAT GRANT US THIS FREEDOM--
SURELY...I HOPE THAT THE MAGIC ISN'T FAILING?
HRMM... THAT WOULD BE TROUBLESOME INDEED.
BUMP

WE SHOULD SEND ONE OF OUR OWN WITH TALA.
TRUE, SCRIBES AT THE SUMMIT MIGHT KNOW MORE. THE STONE IS UP THERE, AFTER ALL...
?

• • !

WE WILL SEND BAE'LI! SHE'S AN EXPERT ON THE TRAIL.
I'M WILLING TO BET IF THERE ARE ANY CLUES AMONGST THE FLORA, SHE WILL FIND THEM.
IN ADDITION, SHE WILL GATHER NEWS FROM THE SUMMIT AND REPORT ON THE STONE.
SHLK
GLP
SLK
SQZ

FWIP
• • •

VERY WELL. TWO TASKS ON ONE PATH.
SEND WORD AS WELL FOR A MEETING OF THE TRIBES AT THE NEXT FULL MOON.
AH, A GOOD PLAN. AGREED, ASKA?
LAP
GLK
HAAAH..
ASKA?
SLRP
H-HAAAH!
Y-YES!
GUH
THUD
HUFF
I-IT'S A G-GOOD PLAN! HAHAH.. HAAAH..
...ALL RIGHT THEN.
?
!
?
?
WE WILL PREPARE. I HOPE THIS URGE DOES NOT BRING US TO HARM BIPEDAL PREY.
hmmm...
WE WILL DEPART AFTER THE CEREMONY.
SMK

ARE YOU READY, TALA?
SSHHH...
...TALA?

Y-YES!
I'M READY!
THE LONG CLIMB!
THE TREK UP DENALI THAT IS TRADITION FOR NEWLY ADULTED TELIDA WOLVES!
Y..YES. WELL—

NO NEED TO BE NERVOUS! YOU'LL MEET BAE'LI IN...A MOMENT. WE'LL GO PREPARE THE CEREMONY FOR YOU.
THE CLIMB IS A GOOD CHANCE TO THINK ABOUT WHAT LIES AHEAD FOR YOU!
KIGA TELLS ME YOU'LL GIVE HIM GOOD PUPS?
SHUFL
SHUFL
W-WHAT?
I NEVER SAID ANYTHING ABOUT THAT!! THAT'S STILL MY CHOICE, RIGHT?
HAH!
SURE, BUT YOU'LL COME TO SEE I'M ALPHA FOR A REASON. THERE'S NO OTHER MALE GOOD ENOUGH IN OUR PACK FOR YOU.
WE'LL BE DOING EACH OTHER A FAVOR!
TSH!

SHUFL
WE WILL SEE YOU OFF SHORTLY.

SNIF

mmm?
THAT'S ROUGH, BUDDY.
GAH!!!
GASP
F-FUCK..!
WOW, YOU MUST HAVE A LOT ON YOUR MIND. FORGOT I WAS HERE?
WANT TO JOIN ME NEXT TIME?
FLAIL
WOBBLE

• • •
WHAT IS ⇥WRONG⇤ WITH YOU?! AFTER EVERYTHING YOU HEARD, ⇥THAT'S⇤ WHAT YOU ASK ME?
HHHNNN
inhale

HAHA, YOU GOT ME THERE! I DIDN'T ACTUALLY HEAR ANYTHING WITH MY MOUTH FULL.
I'M ACTUALLY PRETTY POOR AT MULTI-TASKING.

WELL--
YOUR... ACTS WERE PRETTY DISTRACTING, YOU KNOW...
sigh
AH, CAN'T FOCUS? YOU MUST BE THIS YEAR'S LONE 'LONG CLIMB' WOLF!
YEAH...I'M AN ADULT, BUT I'M BEING HANDLED LIKE A PUP.
IT'S ALL BECAUSE OF WHAT I DO IN THE PACK. FISHING, WEAVING, PAINTING... ANYTHING BUT HUNT.
huff
SO YOU NEED GUTS, JUST NOT PREY GUTS.

ALRIGHT--
SLP
SHUFFLE
LET ME GET THIS STRAIGHT: 'ALPHA' IS JUST WHAT YOU GUYS CALL YOUR CHIEF, RIGHT? IT'S NOT LIKE, A DOMINANCE THING, YEAH?
WELL.. YES...
SO IT'S NOT LAW, RIGHT? CAN'T YOU, I DUNNO, LEAVE? TRUE, YOU'RE AWFULLY, UH...SMALL, AND AS FEROCIOUS AS A FISH--
--BUT YOU GOTTA DO ->SOMETHING<-. THIS 'HUNT' YOU ALL ARE FEELING SOUNDS LIKE IT SUCKS, SO DOING NOTHING PROBABLY ISN'T AN OPTION.
TCH!
Y-YEAH..EVEN EATING FERAL PREY IS GROSS TO ME...
GUT INSTINCT! LITERALLY!
EITHER FIGHT IT OR EMBRACE IT, BUT WHICHEVER YOU PICK, FOLLOW THROUGH!
I MEAN...I DON'T KNOW ANYTHING ABOUT YOU OR YOUR PACK, BUT THAT'S JUST MY TWO BONES.
I SUPPOSE THAT MAKES SENSE...

C'MON, I'M SURE THEY'RE WAITING. I'VE GOT SOME ERRANDS THERE TOO.
YOU DO?
YEAH, I'M KIND OF THE VILLAGE HERBALIST. MY GRANDMA SAID SHE NEEDS SOMETHING.
IT MUST BE NICE TO HAVE A ROLE TO PLAY IN YOUR TRIBE...
EH? DIDN'T YOU SAY YOU DID STUFF IN YOURS?

YEAH...BUT EVER SINCE THIS 'HUNTING URGE' HAS GROWN, EVERYONE SEEMS SO LESS INTERESTED IN THE PEACEFUL THINGS.
OH, RIGHT. I THOUGHT I HEARD SOMETHING ABOUT FORAGED FOODS..? MAYBE YOU COULD MAKE THEM MORE APPETIZING?
YOU KNOW, OFFSET THAT MEAT-ONLY DIET THAT'S PROBABLY NOT GOOD FOR YOUR HEALTH.
I..WOULD LOVE TO TRY THAT, ACTUALLY!

HERE YOU ARE. GOOD LUCK!
THANK YOU...
TALA.
COME.

YOU CAME OF AGE TWO MOONS AGO, AND NOW WILL CLIMB DENALI.
SHFFLE

YOU MAY SEEM WEAK NOW, BUT YOU ARE TELIDA.
YOU HAVE RESOLVE.

WATER FROM THE SUMMIT SPRING, BROUGHT BACK BY THE LAST CLIMB.
YOU WILL BRING YOUR OWN BACK WITH YOU.

FIRE...THAT'S RIGHT. THAT DREAM I HAD...
SHOULD I SAY SOMETHING?
CRACKLE
FIRE FROM THE TREES, WATER FROM THE SNOW, SMOKE IN THE AIR--

DENALI, THE TALL ONE.

OUR SIBLING IN THE URSA TRIBE WILL WALK WITH HER. SHOW THE WAY.

KOFF

KOFF

THESE PARTS OF THE EARTH ARE ALSO PART OF YOU AS A WOLF.

IN YOUR SHADOW, WE WALK UPRIGHT AND SPEAK WITH FORMALITY. HELP US PROTECT THIS BY RETURNING TALA TO US STRONGER.

TALA WILL SEEK HERSELF. BAE'LI WILL SEEK THE FLORA FOR ANY SIGNS OF THIS 'HUNT' AND TO GATHER NEWS FROM--

WHINE

PSSHHHH

FFSHH H

CRACKLE

STIR

W-WAIT--

WHAT?!

IS SOMETHING THE MATTER, MY CHILD?

OH...HI, GRANDMA.

I TRIED NOT TO YELL TOO LOUD... I DIDN'T EVEN SEE YOU THERE. DID YOU GET SHORTER?

HAH! YOU REALLY HAVE THAT SPUNK LIKE YOUR MOTHER!

YOU ALSO HAVE HER NOSE! WE'RE ASKING THAT YOU SNIFF SOMETHING OUT FOR US...

ASKING? OR TELLING.

I MEAN, I DON'T MIND HELPING THE POOR DOG, BUT...REALLY?!
DEAR,
THE TRIBES WANT YOU TO FIND OUT IF THERE'S ANYTHING IN THE FLORA HERE THAT COULD AFFLICT THE WOLVES, AND →I←...
I HAVE A... PRIVATE REQUEST.
WOULD YOU BE A LOVELY CHILD AND KEEP A NOSE OUT...
NOD
SHUFFLE

FOR THESE?
I DON'T KNOW IF OTHERS HAVE NOTICED THEM. THEY ARE QUITE RECENT--I'VE NOT SEEN THEM BEFORE LAST SEASON.
I'VE BEEN SNEAKING OUT AT NIGHT TO GATHER THEM, BUT I THINK--

GRANDMA, SNEAKING OUT AT NIGHT ISN'T SAFE! AND DOESN'T THAT LOOK LIKE 'UNUSUAL FLORA' TO YOU?!
I DON'T THINK THIS IS WHAT THE WOLVES ARE LOOKING FOR.
WHY..?
OH! WELL...IT GIVES ME A GOOD YOUTHFUL ENERGY, AND A.. AHH, HOW YOU SAY, MAKES A NICE...
UMM...
A NICE... WHAT?
LOVE-MAKING OIL...?
...I WISH I COULD UN-HEAR THAT.
SLAP

YOU CAN TAKE MUCH LARGER MALES WITH IT! I MEAN, WHEN I--
GRANDMA!
..PLEASE!

THAT'S WHAT I GET FOR SUCKING DICK DURING A MEETING...
UGH...
H-HEY!
IT'S YOU! BAE'LI..?

BRUSH
HMM? OH...
RIGHT, I GUESS WE NEVER ACTUALLY INTRODUCED EACH OTHER EARLIER.
YEP, THAT'S ME. LOUD BRAT WITH DYED HAIR. HERBALIST. NOT TOO SURPRISED I WAS PICKED.

ANYWAY--
'TALA', WAS IT?
WELL, IT'S 'YOUNG RIVER', BUT 'TALA' IS--
FWIP!
WAH!
MOUNTAIN'S THIS WAY! CAN'T MISS IT!

GET YOUR CUTE ASS MOVING!
WHUFF!
SLAP!

LIKE I SAID EARLIER, YOU HAVE TO BE DECISIVE.
A-ALRIGHT,
BUT DID YOU HAVE TO SLAP MY BUTT?!
YES.
...IN FRONT OF EVERYONE?!
...YYYES?

HOURS INTO THE NIGHT...
--AND THAT'S WHY I'LL NEVER HAVE A MATE. I'M JUST A BIG FLUFFY SHUT-OUT.
AWW.
WHAT ABOUT YOU? GOING TO GO BACK TO KIGA LIKE HE WANTS?
EH...
KIGA ISN'T TERRIBLE, BUT HE'S GOT A LOT TO LEARN IF HE STILL THINKS I'LL HAVE HIS PUPS...
THAT'S THE CONFIDENCE I WAS TALKING ABOUT! MORE OF THAT!
ASKA IS A BIG CUDDLE BEAR, LITERALLY. GOOD LEADER. KIND OF WHY I LIKE 'HELPING' HIM...
YOU COULD'VE JOINED ME!
W-WHAT KIND OF GIRL DO YOU THINK I AM?!
UMM... BORING?
BORING?! I..LIKE SEX!
IT JUST TAKES ME TO KNOW SOMEONE FIRST BEFORE I GO HAVING SEX WITH THEM!
I'VE...ONLY HAD IT A FEW TIMES, BUT IT'S NOT LIKE I DON'T...
...WHAT... ARE YOU DOING?
I'M STILL LISTENING!
I LIKE CLOUDBERRY COLOR, AND THEY'RE LOW ELEVATION, SO, GRABBING SOME BEFORE WE GO ANY HIGHER.
OHH...
WHY DYE IT? IF I CAN ASK?
WAVE
YOU'RE A DOLL.
SAY, WE'RE NEAR A NEAT LITTLE SPOT. KNOW HOW TO SWIM?
SHORT VERSION? GROWING UP, I WAS PICKED ON OFTEN.
FOR SOME REASON THE COLOURS HELP ME FEEL COMFORTABLE.
WHAT?! BUT YOU'RE SO NICE!
hehe
NO, NOT MUCH DEEP WATER BY OUR PACK.

OH THAT'S ALRIGHT. JUST DIP YOUR FEET IN, AT LEAST!
OH! IT'S SO SERENE!
I FOUND IT A WHILE BACK, HELPING ANOTHER WOLF CLIMB.

IT'S SO WARM! WHAT'S THE SECRET?
RRGH!
BEATS ME!
GRR...
O-OOHH...
SPLASH

YOU KNOW,
I THOUGHT I WOULD HATE THIS CLIMB. BUT, IT REALLY HELPS TO GET AWAY FROM THE PACK FOR A WHILE.
AND HAVING SOMEONE TO VENT AND TALK TO ABOUT EVERYTHING THAT'S GOING ON?
WELL, THAT'S JUST A PLEASANT SURPRISE! SO, THANK YOU BAE'LI...
SPLASH

YOU'VE BEEN--
SPLASH
HEY!

WHY THANK YOU, LITTLE WOLF, BUT IT'S TIME TO UNWIND SOME--
OR DO I HAVE TO MAKE YOU?

MAKE ME? HOW--
WUFF
!?
C'MON, YOU CAN'T BE THAT OBLIVIOUS.
I THINK YOU'D ENJOY A CHANGE FROM ALL OF THE MALES...
I-I...
YOU WHAT?
I SAW YOUR FACE FROM UNDERNEATH THE TABLE. BLUSHING, INTRIGUED!
THERE'S NOTHING MORE INTRIGUING THAN TRYING NEW THINGS...
TSK
AND I GUARANTEE BEARS HAVE LARGE TONGUES FOR A GOOD REASON OR TWO.
YOU CAN SAY 'NO', OF COURSE. I WON'T TAKE OFFENSE.
SPLISH
SIGH
HEHE, MAYBE I AM CURIOUS, I JUST DIDN'T EXPECT...
ME NEITHER! YOU'VE GROWN ON ME RATHER QUICKLY THOUGH.
SO IF I CAN HELP DE-STRESS YOU...

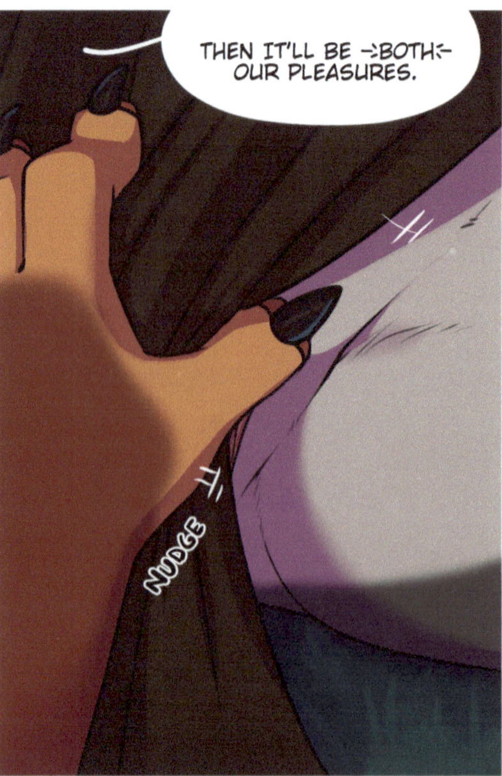
THEN IT'LL BE ⇒BOTH⇐ OUR PLEASURES.
NUDGE

chehe...
S-SURE!

YOU SMELL CUTE.
C-COLD NOSE...
Y-YOU'RE REALLY... DOING IT, HUH?
THAT F-FEELS..
AH!
NUZZLE
AHHHH..!
SHLP!
AH.. HAH
SHIVER
AH..HAH..
I'VE NEVER BEEN L..LICKED...
ESPECIALLY DAY ONE.
MMN?
DON'T MIND ME IF I GIVE YOU A BIT MORE OF IT, THEN.
SSHHHLRP!
HHAAH!
SHLCK
SHLRP
SHLP
MMH~

HA-
WHUFF
-AH!
HUFF
PANT
Y-YOU'RE REALLY NOT GOING E-EASY ON ME..!
FFF-FUCK..!
MMH!
LAP
LAP
LAP
LAP
SHLRP
SHLK
HAA-
HAH-
SLP
SCRRRGH
F-FUCK...
COULD SHE REALLY TELL HOW CURIOUS I WAS?
HER TONGUE IS SO THICK AND SQUIRMING...
HAH...
HUFF..
AH..

ACTUALLY... HERE, I HAVE A BETTER SEAT FOR YOU--
A...WHA-?
H-HEY!
WUFF
FLAIL
AH..!
H-HAAH-- HAAAAAAH!
HAAAH~
LICK
LAP
R-RELENTLESS TONGUE..!!
YOU REALLY WANT MY... HONEY, BEAR?!
HAH!
LAP
LAP
AAAAH~!
FLICK
HNNGH~
SLLP
SLP
THERE WE GO! IN CUTE-BUTT-GRABBING RANGE!
GRIP
LAP
LICK
OOOOH-
SLLLLLRRP!
-GAWDS...
SHLP

I'M..GONNA CUM LIKE THIS..!
NNNN...
TELL ME TALA,
ARE BEAR FINGERS THICKER THAN WOLF FINGERS?
PRESS~
HUH?! I...I--
HH
SSSSHLCK!
SSLIP
I KNOW ALL THE RIGHT ANGLES TO AVOID THE CLAWS--
HAAA HH!
I'M...
CUMMING!
LAP
LAP
LAP
SLP
SHLK
GRIP
SLP
GOOD GIRL.
LAP
HOW STRANGE...
IN THIS MOMENT, THE LIGHTS LOOK SO...
HAH
HUFF
...HEAVY...
HA...

NNGH...
...WHAT...
...IS HAPPENING...
...TO ME?

...WAIT.
SNIF
I CAN SUDDENLY SMELL...
...MORE?
SNIF
SNIF

I CAN HEAR MORE, TOO...
bzzzzzzzz
...TINY THINGS, FAR AWAY...

LIKE...MY HEAD IS... SEARCHING FOR SOMETHING FAR OFF...
splsh

AH...!
I'VE FOUND IT!
HAH
...PREY!
HUFF

CROUCH
HNH?
TALA, ARE YOU--
GRIP

O...
...KAY?
LEAP

FWISH-
DASH
DASH

ERM...
DID I GO TOO FAST?

TALA!

SKSH
SKSH
DASH
HERE!
THWUMP!
WHAT A STRONG SCENT...AND FROM SO FAR AWAY..!
MY PREY IS RIGHT HERE!
I'LL PROVE I CAN HUNT. I'M A FULL-FANGED WOLF.
A PREDATOR...

CHOMP
GOT YOU!

?

HNNH?
WAIT... THIS--
HE'S--

ACK!
WOOSH
-HUGE!

AH!

NGH!
THUD

SO...

DO I BITE YOU NOW?

NNH...
...SNRK-
-PF-
HA!
AHAH!
AHAHA
S-SORRY..! I COULD NOT RESIST-- HA!
I'M SURPRISED THAT I CAME UP WITH THAT SO SWIFTLY!
haha...
O-OH GOSH!
YOU.. YOU'RE OKAY?
ARE YOU HURT?
HURT?
GOODNESS NO, YOU'RE MUCH TOO SMALL--PROBABLY HOW YOU SNUCK UP ON ME!
AND I MEAN NO OFFENSE, BUT YOUR 'FANGS' ARE MORE AKIN TO PEBBLES!
I AM QUITE ALRIGHT, BUT THANK YOU!
YOU TOOK A LITTLE FALL THERE, ARE ->YOU<- ALRIGHT?

...PEBBLE TEETH?

W-WAIT! I ATTACKED YOU!!
I DON'T ATTACK ANYONE, EVEN FERALS!!
I DON'T EVEN KNOW-- JUST THE LIGHTS, AND THEN...!

KIIGUYAT... THE SPIRITS; OUR ANCESTORS.
MY HERD SHAMAN HAS CALLED UPON THEM IN TRANCE, BUT...
THIS WOULD BE THE FIRST TIME I'VE HEARD OF THEM -:CAUSING:- ONE.
WH..WHY THEN..?
I ADMIT I'M NOT SURE...
YOU SAID YOU DON'T WISH TO HUNT EVEN BEAST PREY? QUITE UNLIKE A WOLF!

SNIF-
FIRST KIGA, NOW EVEN MY ANCESTORS ARE TRYING TO CONTROL ME?!
SNIF
HOLD ON NOW...

I MAY BE ABLE TO HELP! BUT FIRST,
I DIDN'T MEAN TO DOUBT YOUR TEETH--
MAYBE YOU'RE PART SHEEP!

?
AH-HA!
YOU KNOW, I WOULDN'T PUT IT PAST ME!
heheh-
IT'S...NOT ABOUT THE TEETH, SILLY!
SNRK
WAS THAT EVEN FUNNY..?
OKAY MAYBE A LITTLE...

I'M GLAD I HAVEN'T LOST ⇁ALL⇃ OF MY SOCIAL SKILLS UP HERE ALONE!
DZAANH NEZOONH!* MY NAME IS MASSAK.
MY N--CALL ME TALA!
*=GREETINGS

WELL TALA,
I CAN'T SPEAK FOR WOLVES, BUT IN OUR HERD, SPIRITS TEACH US HOW TO IMPROVE AND EVOLVE, SEPARATING US FROM FERAL FORMS.
IF WOLVEN SPIRITS WERE TRYING TO GET YOU TO KILL... YOU'RE PRETTY SPECIAL FOR BREAKING FREE!
DON'T FLATTER ME ⇁TOO⇃ MUCH, MISTER. I'M NOT AN ANGEL...
YOU'RE SPECIAL TOO! RAMS I'VE SEEN VISIT OUR PACK WERE MEAGER...
...LIKE ME.
HAH! ONE DOES BUILD UP STRENGTH LIVING UP HERE BY YOURSELF!

eh?
YOU LIVE HERE?
OHO!*
SOMEONE HAS TO! THE SOUTH PEAK OF IS WHERE EAGLES FROM TACOMA BRING NEWS FROM AFAR.
I STUDIED FOR YEARS, BUT ONLY RECENTLY TOOK UP THE POST.
SO IT WAS YOU THAT RELAYED THE RECENT NEWS TO US!
ASTUTE!
WORK HERE IS TRANSCRIBING, RESEARCHING, FORAGING...
Crackle
*=YES INDEED

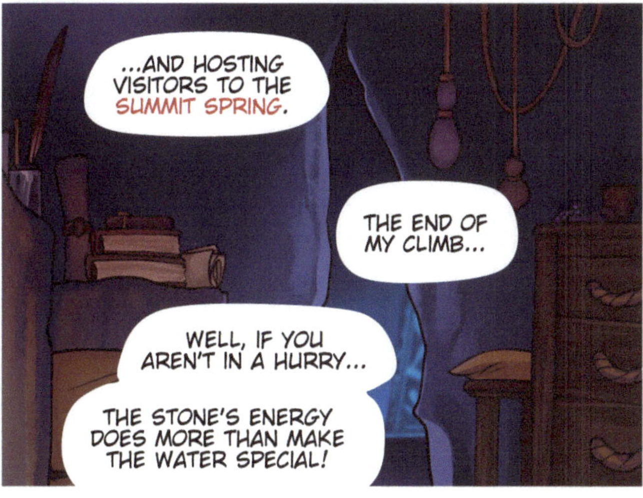

...AND HOSTING VISITORS TO THE SUMMIT SPRING.
THE END OF MY CLIMB...
WELL, IF YOU AREN'T IN A HURRY...
THE STONE'S ENERGY DOES MORE THAN MAKE THE WATER SPECIAL!

IT'S LED TO NEW DISCOVERIES SUCH AS THESE 'ROCK STICKS' CALLED 'IRON'--
'UNMELTING ICE' WE CALL 'GLASS'!
POTENT ALCHEMICAL MIXES WITH SPECIAL PROPERTIES FROM NEW FRUITS!
hehe
IT'S CUTE, A BIG GUY LIKE YOU INTO ALL THAT,
BUT...IS IT REALLY JUST YOU UP HERE?
Snap
chk

WELL, WHEN THE EAGLES RELAY NEWS FROM TACOMA, THEY... KEEP ME IN GOOD COMPANY...
GOT SEED FOR THIS BIRD, MASSAK?
--BUT ENOUGH ABOUT THEM!
WAVE
I ENJOY ALL VISITORS! ARE YOU ALONE AS WELL?
OH!
NO, I SET OUT WITH A FRIEND, AND I JUST RAN OFF...
I JUST HOPE SHE'S ALRIGHT--IT'S FREEZING! SHEESH, EVEN WITH FUR, CLOTHES AND FIRE!
ONE OF THE BEARS?
SHIVER
SHIVER
YEAH...
THE URSA TRIBE ARE TOUGH; I THINK SHE'LL BE OKAY!
HERE...

THIS SHOULD WARM YOU UP!
WH-
WHAT IS...
SOUP! I ADMIT IT LOOKS A LITTLE UNNATURAL...
THE BEAN I USE IS NEW HERE. IT HAS SOME VARIOUS BENEFICIAL, AND DELICIOUS, EFFECTS.

WARMTH, CALMNESS... EVEN THE EAGLES SAID IT BROUGHT CLARITY!
IT'S A LITTLE DIFFERENT FOR EVERYONE, BUT--
GIP!
OH.
THAT WAS QUICK!
haaa...

NEVER WAS MUCH OF A COOK, BUT UP HERE ALONE, YOU HAVE TO PRACTICE!
I HOPE IT'S PASSABLE?

...OOBOOHOH~!
I DIDN'T KNOW HOW MUCH I NEEDED THIS!!
huff
GOSH, JUST MATE ME!

AHAH!--
...YOU...WHAT?

OH BOY HOW I WISH I COULD VANISH RIGHT THIS MOMENT
DID I REALLY JUST SAY THAT?
JUST A SHEEP
MORE IMPORTANTLY, DID I REALLY MEAN IT
WHAT ARE YOU THINKING TALA, THE WOLVES WOULD KILL YOU
WHEN DID I GET SO FORWARD?
I REALLY WANT SOME AFFECTION
BURY MY FACE INTO HIS FUR
DADDY
ARE SHEEP SUPPOSED TO BE HOT?
HAVE I ALWAYS BEEN
WHY AM I BURNING UP DOWN THERE?
IF ANYTHING I SHOULD WANT TO HUNT HIM, RIGHT?
I MEAN HE'S CUTE BUT HE'S PREY
HIS SCENT IS SO CALMING
I BET HIS DICK IS HU
ARE HIS BALLS SOFT LIKE THE REST OF HIS FUR
WANT TO GRAB HIS HORNS AND RIDE

A-HAHA!
ha ha
I MEANT, THIS COULD REALLY SAVE MY BUTT!
I'D NEVER HAVE TO HUNT AT ALL! BETWEEN FISHING AND STUFF LIKE THIS--!

heheh
I MUST SAY, I'VE MET PLENTY OF WOLVES HERE ON THEIR ASCENT...
YOU ARE QUITE DIFFERENT!
BUT THAT... BOREAL TRANCE MUST HAVE TAKEN ITS TOLL ON YOU.

THERE'S A GUEST SPOT HERE I'LL PREPARE--
I MADE IT MYSELF!

O...
OKAY...
DAMMIT, TALA!
I FELT LIKE I MEANT IT...
SO WHY'D I TAKE IT BACK?!
HE'S BIG, CUTE, AND I'M FINALLY OUT OF KIGA'S REACH...
...
YOU KNOW WHAT, KIGA? I THINK I WILL, FOR ONCE...
HUNT!

...BUT HUNT IN MY OWN WAY.

'MASSAK', WAS IT? I--

AH! J-JUST A MOMENT!

..O-OH.

MY APOLOGIES! THIS WOOL'S RATHER FLAT, HAH!

JUST PREPARING A GUEST SPACE FOR YOU! I'D RATHER IT NOT BE SUCH A RUN-DOWN MESS.

I NEED A SHEARING ANYWAY, SO IF YOU--

W-WAIT!

!?

STOP!!

KEEP YOUR FUR! I'LL JUST... SLEEP HERE...

FWUMP

ARE... ARE YOU SURE YOU'RE ALRIGHT, TALA?

SO...SOFF...

S-SORRY.
I KNOW THIS
PROBABLY SEEMS
SILLY-
AND I ONLY
JUST MET YOU!
OH, IT'S
QUITE ALRIGHT!
YOU SEEM GOOD-
NATURED, JUST...
UNDER STRESS?
YOU GOT
THAT RIGHT...
THERE'S SOME
THINGS I WANT,
AS A PREDATOR.
AS A LADY.
I'M PUSHING
MYSELF TO
JUST...TAKE IT!

AND...
heh
WHAT...IS IT THAT
YOU WANT?

REALLY?
JUST HAVE TO MAKE ME
SAY IT OUT LOUD, HUH?

MEAT.

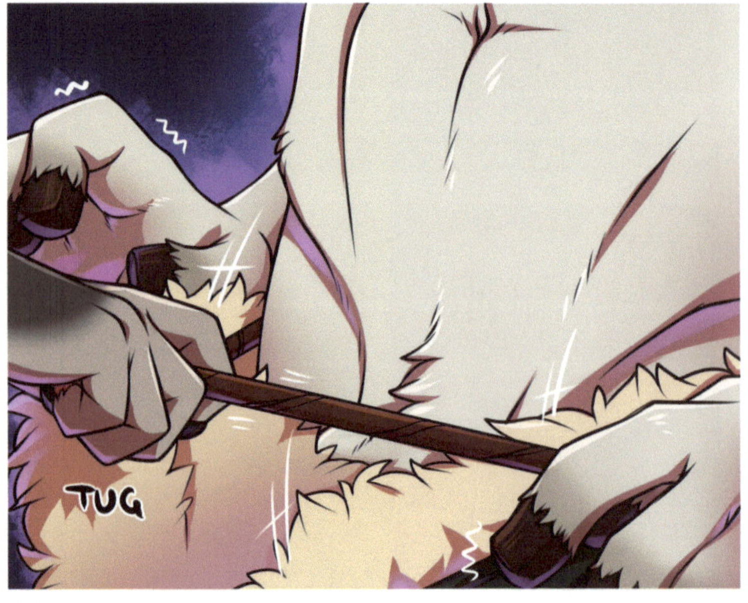
TUG

UHM...
I—...
WHAT'S WRONG, LITTLE WOLF? YOU WERE SO CONFIDENT!
YOU'RE...
BIG.
GET YOUR LITTLE MAW IN THERE,
AND LET'S GET YOU FED.
MNF!
H-HAH
O-
OKAY...
H-HAH

WELL...THAT'S ONE REASON I HESITATED,
BUT IF YOU'RE HUNGRY ENOUGH TO TRY THIS "MEAT" ANYWAY...
Y-YES!
SORRY, I SOUND SILLY WHEN HORN-- ...HUNGRY.
WELL THEN-
!?

NUZZLE
SNF
HAH
HUFF

IT'S DRAWING ME IN...
HE'S SO WARM.
BRUSH
THIS HEAVY AND DOMINANT SCENT...
...CLEAN AND COMPELLING...
SNF
HUFF
...SATURATED WITH IT.
HAH
HAH
heh-
GOSH, I MUST LOOK DESPERATE.
A WOLF DRAWN TO A SHEEP--
UNHEARD OF!
QUITE ALRIGHT, TALA. I WAS WORRIED YOU WERE NOT OF CLEAR MIND. AND 'UNHEARD OF'?
-Y-YOU REALLY DO FLATTER ME WITH THIS... I'M ONLY PREY.
SHIVER
HFF
HAH..
NO, YOU'RE HEAVENLY~!
PLEASE, LET ME-- JUST THIS ONCE!

'LET YOU'?
IF YOU DESIRE THIS, TALA, I WON'T--
...STOP YOU.
NGH-
PUSH
STOP?! NO...
HUFF
HA
I NEED...
A TASTE!
HAAAAH~
SLRP
MMH-!
hehheh
WELL THAT WAS A PLEASANT GREETING.
I HOPE THAT ISN'T ALL...
...DOES THE LITTLE WOLF WANT THE FULL MEAL?
NOD NOD
NUZZLE

YOU MAY NEED BOTH PAWS...
WAG
GRIP
NGH
I DON'T EXPECT YOU TO TAKE ME WHOLE,
BUT YOU'RE READY TO TRY?
NOD
MH-HM!
HEHEH, ALRIGHT.
WHINE
HUFF
Q-QUITE WARM, YOU ARE...

MNNN-
AND ALTHOUGH SNUG...
HAAH...
...I MAY JUST BE...
-HA A A...
TOO BIG?
hehe
keheh

BUT PERHAPS...
THIS OIL, IT'S MADE FROM THE SAME BEAN SEEDS I USED FOR THE SOUP--
hehe
MASSAK...
I KNOW IT MAY SEEM SILLY!
hmmm...
I'M FAMILIAR WITH PRESSING OIL FROM SEEDS, I JUST DON'T SEE HOW --ANY-- OIL COULD HELP YOU...'FIT'?
HEH!
EXACTLY! AS THE SOUP, WITH ITS PROPERTIES, WAS NOT JUST ANY SOUP,
THIS IS NOT JUST JUST ANY OIL!
JUST DON'T ASK ME HOW I KNOW IT WORKS.
KNEAD
RUB
YOU'LL STILL TASTE ME QUITE WELL IF YOU--
NGH~
I'LL TAKE THAT AS A YES.
OKAY LITTLE WOLF, DON'T FORGET TO BREATHE...
HAAAAAH...
GRIP
THROB
AH-H...✷
SLP

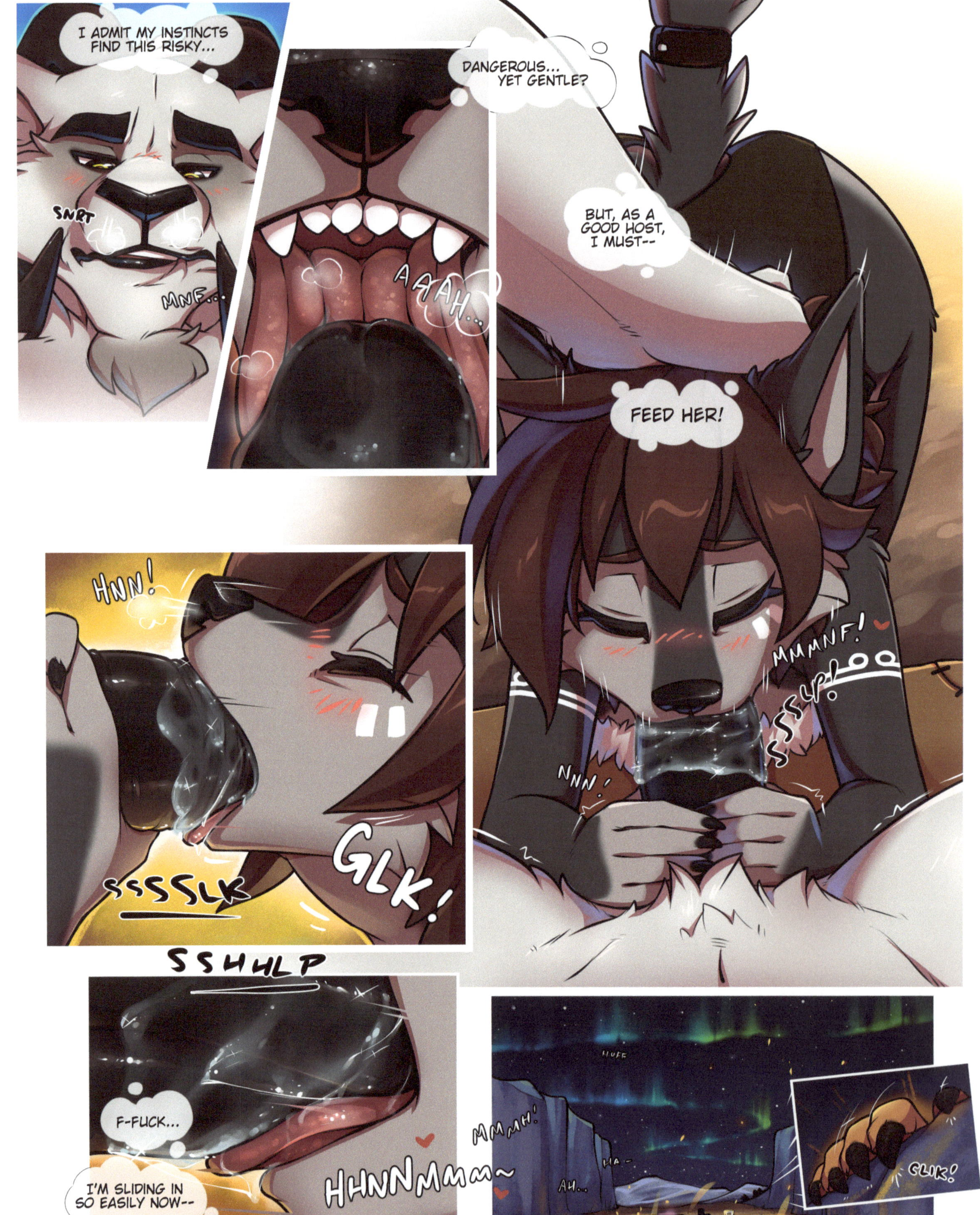
I ADMIT MY INSTINCTS FIND THIS RISKY...
SNRT
MNF...
AAAH...
DANGEROUS... YET GENTLE?
BUT, AS A GOOD HOST, I MUST--
FEED HER!
HNN!
SSSSLK
GLK!
MMMNF!
SSSLPP!
NNN!
SSHULP
F-FUCK...
I'M SLIDING IN SO EASILY NOW--
HHNNMMM~
MMMH!
HA--
AH...
HUFF
CRACKLE
POP
GLIK!

TALA-!
HUFF
HUFF
HUFF
YOU BETTER BE UP HERE!

JUST TILT YOUR HEAD BACK A LITTLE...
TH-THERE, WOLF...
HFF
HFF
SLAP
SLP
SMAK
TALA?
ARE YOU...
HFF
SMACK
SLAP
PLAP
SMACK

PINCH ME IF I GO TOO--
SLLP...
HNNN...
--DEEP!
HNGH!

-SLAP!
GLLP!

SMACK
AHN, THAT'S ALL THE WAY DOWN-- HNNGH
H..HUNGRY GIRL, AREN'T YOU?
HOLY SHEEP!
TWACK
SWISH
SLAP
SNRT!
HUFF
GLK!
PLAP
THUD
MHF!
SLP
SMACK
YOU'RE QUITE WET, TOO... HUFF!

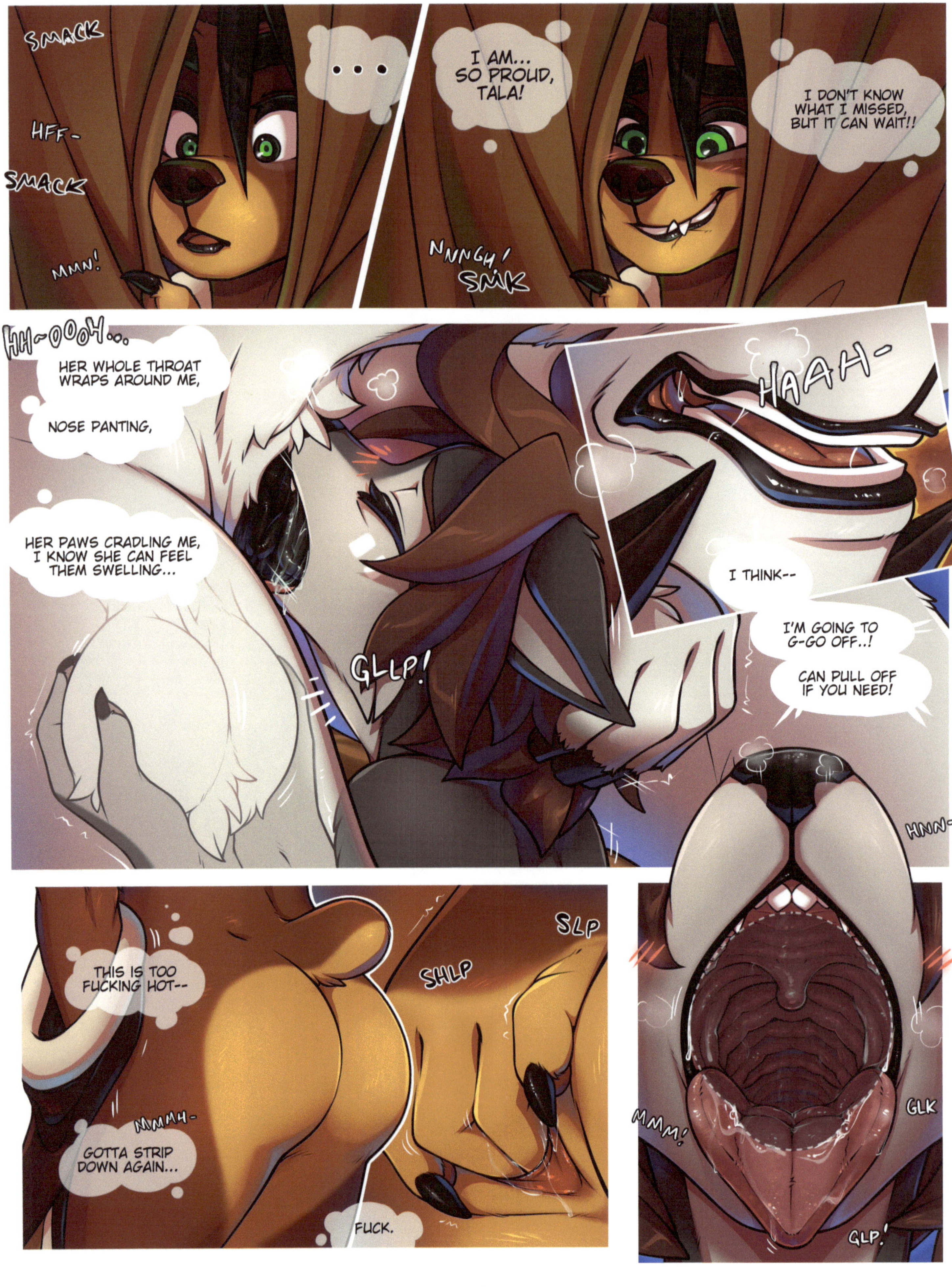

SMACK
HFF-
SMACK
MMN!
. . .
I AM... SO PROUD, TALA!
I DON'T KNOW WHAT I MISSED, BUT IT CAN WAIT!!
NNNGH! SMK

HH-OOOH...
HER WHOLE THROAT WRAPS AROUND ME,
NOSE PANTING,
HER PAWS CRADLING ME, I KNOW SHE CAN FEEL THEM SWELLING...
GLLP!
HAAH-
I THINK--
I'M GOING TO G-GO OFF..!
CAN PULL OFF IF YOU NEED!
HNN-

THIS IS TOO FUCKING HOT--
MMMH-
GOTTA STRIP DOWN AGAIN...
FUCK.
SHLP
SLP
MMM!
GLK
GLP!

HNNH
T-TALA...
G-GONNA →
HHH~
SPLT!
THROB
PULSE
GH-
GH-HAAAAAHH!!!
GLP
GLK
HUFF
OH FUCK ME...
HUFF
SHLP
THROB
NGH-
GULP
SPLT
SPLT
GULP
H-O-OH FFFUCK...
GULP
GLK
GLP

GLLK
GHLP
GHLK

MMMH!
PLP
SPLT
SHLP

GASP
SPLT

SPLRT
SPLT
GHHHLP!
MMMNN...

FWIP
SWISH

HHHFF
FFF
FF
HH~
HAAHH...

HEHE...
HFF
HUFF
HMM?
I DON'T REALLY... GET TO DO THIS STUFF.
S-SORRY...
HAH! TALA, I DON'T JUDGE YOU.
→I← SHOULD BE APOLOGIZING! I MADE A MESS OF YOU AFTER JUST THE FIRST GO!
SCRITCH
FIRST?! OF HOW MANY?
...ERR... 'A LOT'?
YOU ARE TOO MUCH PREY FOR THIS ONE PREDATOR, MISTER!
LAP
WELL...
IF IT'S NOT TOO BOLD OF ME...
...I DON'T THINK YOUR BEAR FRIEND AT THE DOOR WOULD MIND HELPING YOU?

?
FRIEND...

ACK
!

H...
Hiiiiiii..
A-HAH! HELLO!

BAE^LI!

YOU'RE OKAY!
I WAS REALLY WORRIED!!
O-OH!
I'M FINE, PUP! SURPRISED YOU MADE IT ALL THE WAY UP HERE SO FAST!
I'M SO SORRY!!
I DON'T KNOW WHAT CAME OVER ME!

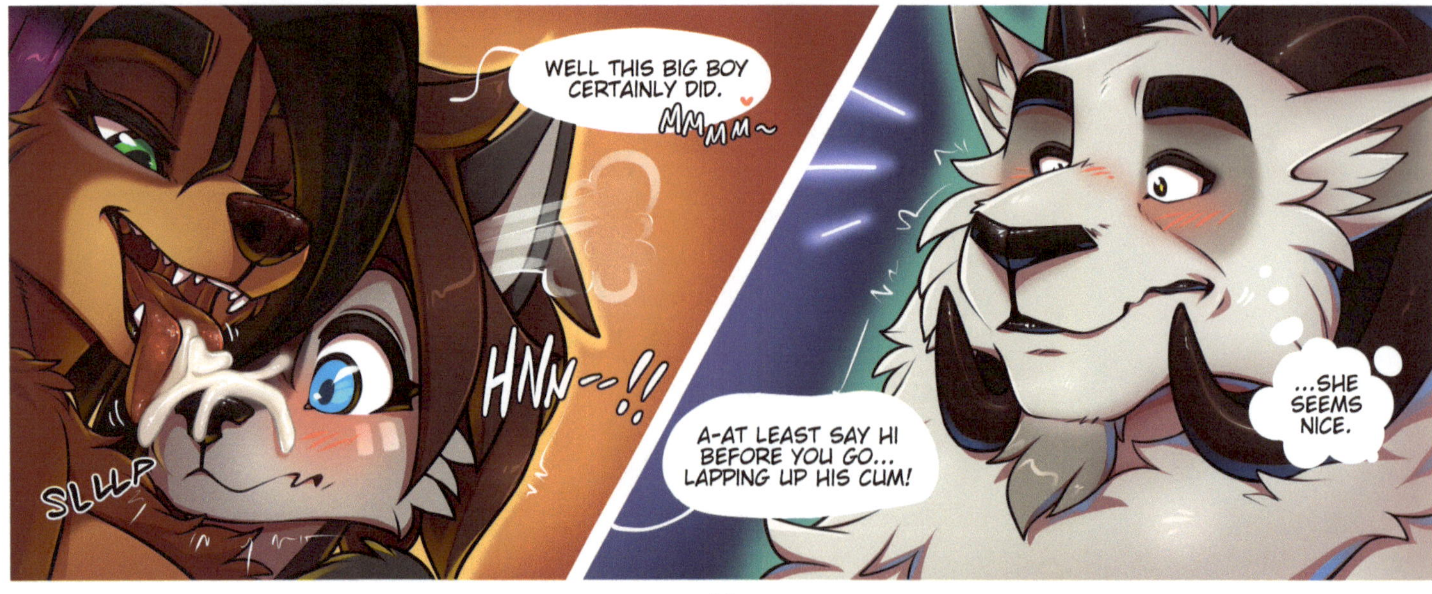
WELL THIS BIG BOY CERTAINLY DID.
MMMM~
HNN~~!!
SLLLP
A-AT LEAST SAY HI BEFORE YOU GO... LAPPING UP HIS CUM!
...SHE SEEMS NICE.

I DID SAY HE WAS TOO MUCH FOR ME ALONE...
HE LOOKS TOUGH, BUT HE'S A BIG SOFTIE- LITERALLY!
'TOUGH'?!
HE COULD FUCK ME INTO HIBERNATION!
SCRITCH
A-HE HEH-!
YOU AAARE... QUITE THE URSINE, MISS BAE'LI!
YOU CAN CALL ME MASSAK!
I'D RATHER CALL YOU DADDY...
AND, WELL, TALA WAS CAUGHT IN SOME KIND OF TRANCE...
I THINK HER AVERSION TO HUNTING MADE HER SUSCEPTIBLE TO SOME KIND...
...OF...
OH DON'T STOP!
I JUST WANT TO GET A GOOD LOOK AT YOU BEFORE WE, WELL, YOU KNOW...
...DEVOUR YOU?
hehe
--IN A GOOD WAY THOUGH!
YOU KNOW OUR TRIBES LOVE TO SHARE.
AND DON'T THINK I'M DONE WITH YOU...

NOW MOVE THAT HAND, SILLY!
I.-ERR..!
YOU'VE BEEN SO CONFIDENT UNTIL NOW, SHEEPIE!
heh!
IT'S JUST... THE FASTEST I'VE GONE FROM 'SAYING HI' TO 'MOUTH ON DICK'...
AND MUCH SHARPER TEETH, I ADMIT...
YEAH! LET ME...
OH
FUCK
SSSLRP.
MMMMᴹH...
THIS SHEEP COCK SMELLS AND TASTES QUITE NICE, YOU KNOW...
NNNH..
L-LADIES...
SHLK
SHLP
SNRL
LAP
MFF
SHLRP
MMMH
SHLLP.
LP
PLP
HAAH...
HUFF
NGH
HUFF
WUFF... I WANT TO GET YOUR SCENT ON ME...
HAAAA...
RUB
- RUB
DROOL...
HUFF
HUFF
HUFF
Y-YEAH, I'M GONNA NEED TO TASTE THIS.

NNH, C'MERE...
SLLLP
SSHLP!
MMNN..
GLK
LET ME SUCK THAT MUSK OFF OF YA...
A - HH - AAAAAH -
HA
AH
SHLK
NNHGH
SHLRP
GLP
GLK
MNN -
H..HEY, MASSAK...
I'VE HAD ENOUGH WAITING AND WONDERING ABOUT THIS...
H-HUFF.
NGH..
...AM I PREDATOR ENOUGH FOR PREY LIKE YOU?
AH~!
HEHEH, WE'RE GOING TO FIND OUT, AREN'T WE?
SQUEEZE
(FIRM BUT GENTLE!)
MM-HMMN~

HFF
HNN...
AH...
WI—
THAT IS,
IF YOUR FRIEND
HERE DOESN'T MAKE
ME BURST AGAIN
ALREADY...
SHUDDER
HEHE, BELIEVE ME,
AS MUCH AS I WANT
A LOAD ALL TO MYSELF,
ALL I'M DOING--
NNN...
SHLLLP
SMK
SLK-
MMMH~
GLLP
SHLK
NGH-
-HFF
HWAH-
HUHFF..
HA~
HA..
HAH
TWITCH
...IS GETTIN' YOU
GOOD AND READY
FOR HER!
I LOVE
EVERYTHING
ABOUT THIS.
I HAVE -:GOT:-
TO SEE IT
THROUGH!
THROB
WELL,
IF HE
ACTUALLY
FITS...
hehe
WIGGLE
WHAT'CHA
SAY, SHEEPIE?

AREN'T I STILL ...'TOO BIG'?
IF YOU WERE, I DON'T THINK I COULD'VE FIT YOU DOWN MY THROAT!
I THINK THAT OIL REALLY DID DO SOMETHING--
BESIDES, BAE'LI WANTS TO HELP TOO!
hehe...

HEHEH, IS THAT SO, BAE'LI?
YEESS!

GRIP
AH!
SPREAD
FUCK...
THAT'S A GOOD VIEW.

ALRIGHT FLUFFY BOY,
NOW I'M →YOUR← PREY.
YES MA'AM, LITTLE WOLF...

SMOOCH-
NUDGE
SLP
MMF-
HA-
FHHUH!!
HA-
HAH!
HA
HUFF
AH-
AHN-
SLP
PLP
PLOP!
!
SHLK
SPLP

THIS. IS. PERFECT.
THE SPLASH ZONE!
SLP
SMAK
SHLK
PLP
THIS RAM'S NO JOKE—
SHLK
PAP
PLP
PLAP
POOR GIRL CAN'T EVEN TAKE IT ALL!
SMAK
TIME TO LEND A HAND...

GRIP
HN-NGH-
THAT'S A NEW FEELING, H-HEH...
SLK
SHLK
SHLP
SHLK
SQZ
SOON AS HE STARTS TO BLOW, THESE ARE GOING BACK IN MY MOUTH...
AH!
IS...SOMETHING WRONG?
WHUFF.
HUFF
HA
HAH
AM I OKAY?!
OH, NO— NOT YOU, TALA.
AH
BAE'LI... GRIPPING ME--
I THINK SHE WANTS TO FEEL ME UNLOAD...
YES!
PLEASE!!
HUFF
FUCK
AH

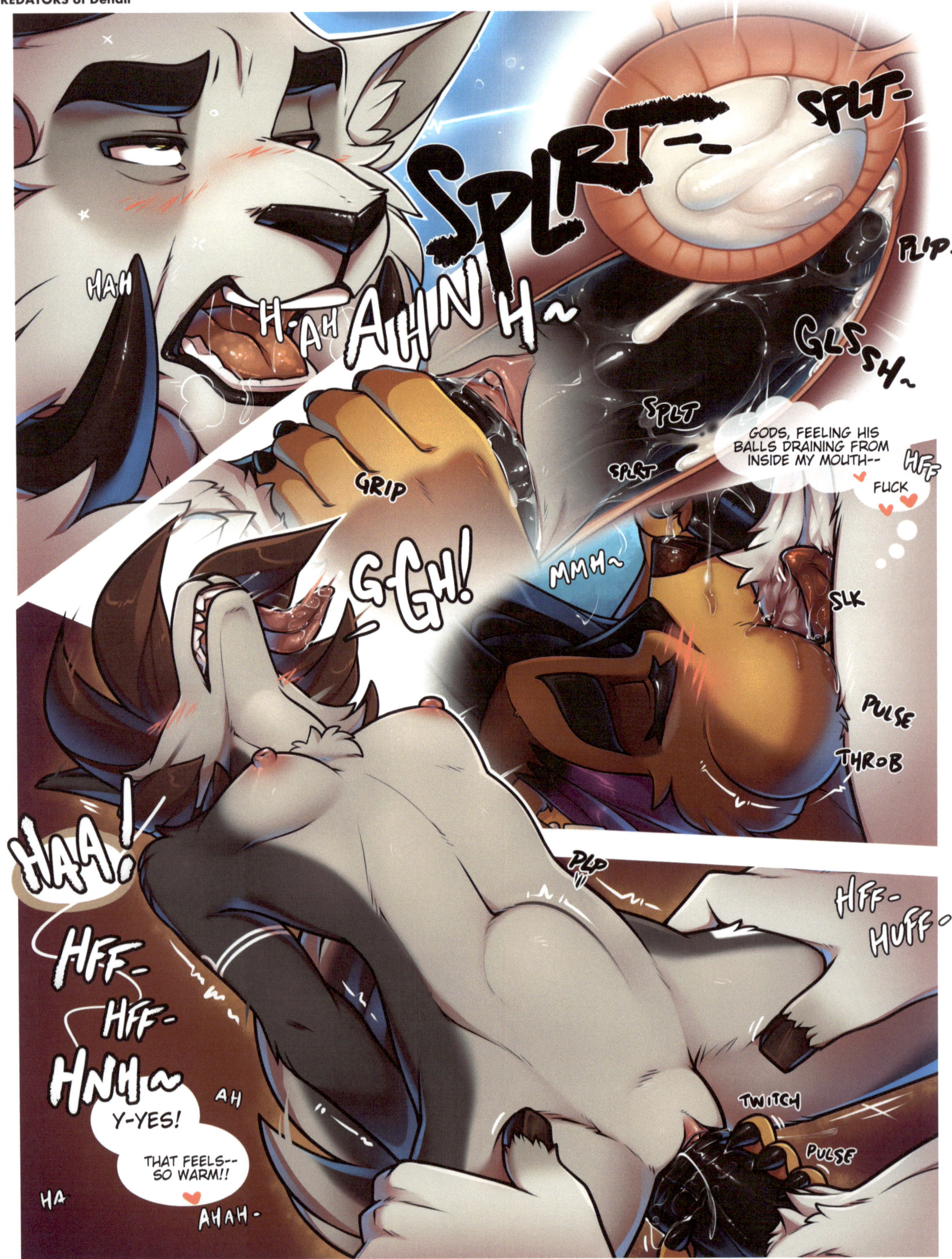
SPLRT--
SPLT-
PLIP.
GLSSH~
HAH
H-AH AHN H~
SPLT
SPLT
MMH~
GRIP
G-GH!
GODS, FEELING HIS
BALLS DRAINING FROM
INSIDE MY MOUTH--
HFF
FUCK
SLK
PULSE
THROB
HAA!
HFF-
HFF-
HNH~
AH
Y-YES!
THAT FEELS--
SO WARM!!
HA
AHAH-
PLP
HFF-
HUFF-
TWITCH
PULSE

A-HAH... PANT
SO THAT'S WHAT THAT FEELS LIKE...
PANT
HFF
HUFF
HAH

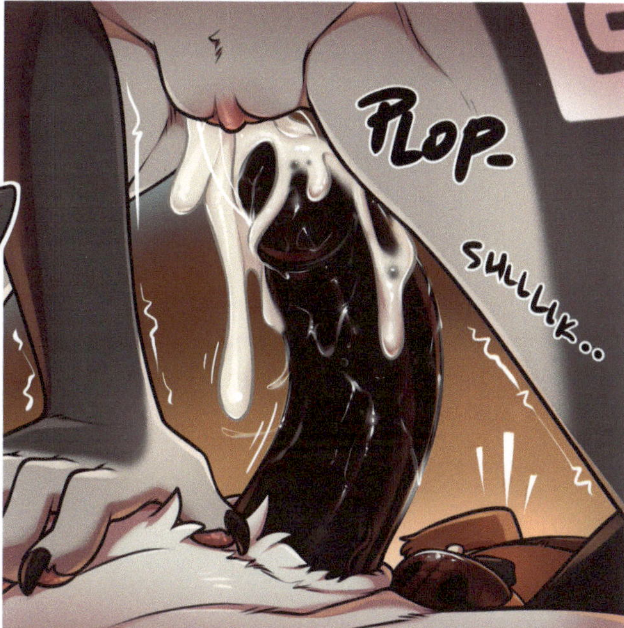
FLOP.
SULLIK..

SMAK!
-MMF!

ARE YOU GIRLS ALWAYS THIS--
POP!
NGH!
GASP!

...THIS 'OUTGOING'?
SHIVER
HUFF
SNRT

...NO.
AT LEAST NOT WITH PREY...
WHAT'D YOU DO?!
SLP
MMMN
HUFF
HUFF
'DO'? HEHEH!
YOUR FRIEND HERE CAME UPON ME, TEETH BARED!
ONCE SHE SNAPPED OUT OF IT, WELL--
MUST HAVE BEEN AWFULLY PENT-UP TO BE THIS...EAGER?
SIGH
AHAH, YEAH, YOU COULD SAY THAT.
WELL...
I HOPE THAT BREW IS FOR STAMINA,
'CAUSE THIS PREDATOR IS HUNGRY TOO.
GULP
MM-HMM!
HEHE, SO QUICK TO AGREE!
SO YOU JUST MIGHT NEED THAT ENERGY...
SWISH

AFTER ->THAT<- GREETING? HOW COULD I NOT!
MMN, GOOD!
FUCK, YOU'VE GOT A GOOD SHAPE...
SQUISH
AND I ->HAD<- TO TASTE YOU. I'VE NEVER HAD PREY LIKE...THAT.
SLP
SHLK
THINK YOU CAN HANDLE HER, MISTER?
SHE MAY BE A BIT MORE WILD.
MM
OH HE HAS NO CHOICE.
haha-
I WILL DO MY BEST! IT'S JUST--
TYPICALLY, ATTRACTION DOESN'T CROSS THAT PREDATOR/PREY LINE...
OH, I'M DEFINITELY CROSSING IT.
CROSSING AND TAKING A SEAT--
HNNGH-- O-O-OF!
H-HG-GH!
SPLRT
SHLAP!
DO IT!

PIFF
THUMP!
HAAAAH!
AAAH~
HA
AH
MMNH-
BLESS THE SPIRITS, FLUFFY BOY! WITH YOUR SHAPE AND SIZE...
FFUCK
I CAN FEEL YOU PUSHIN' MY--
BUMP
--INSIDES AROUND. HOOO-OH!
HUFF
JUST LET MY WEIGHT PUSH IT IN DEEP...
SHLP
PLAP
SHLK
WIGGLE
MMN, SO SNUG.
RUB RUB
NOW LET'S RIDE!
SHLAK
HUFF
IF YOU LADIES K-KEEP THIS PACE-- MORE...SEEDS!
HFF
YES!
ON IT!
HAH
HAAA-
MY DICK'S SO... SWALLOWED UP!
SLP
PLAP

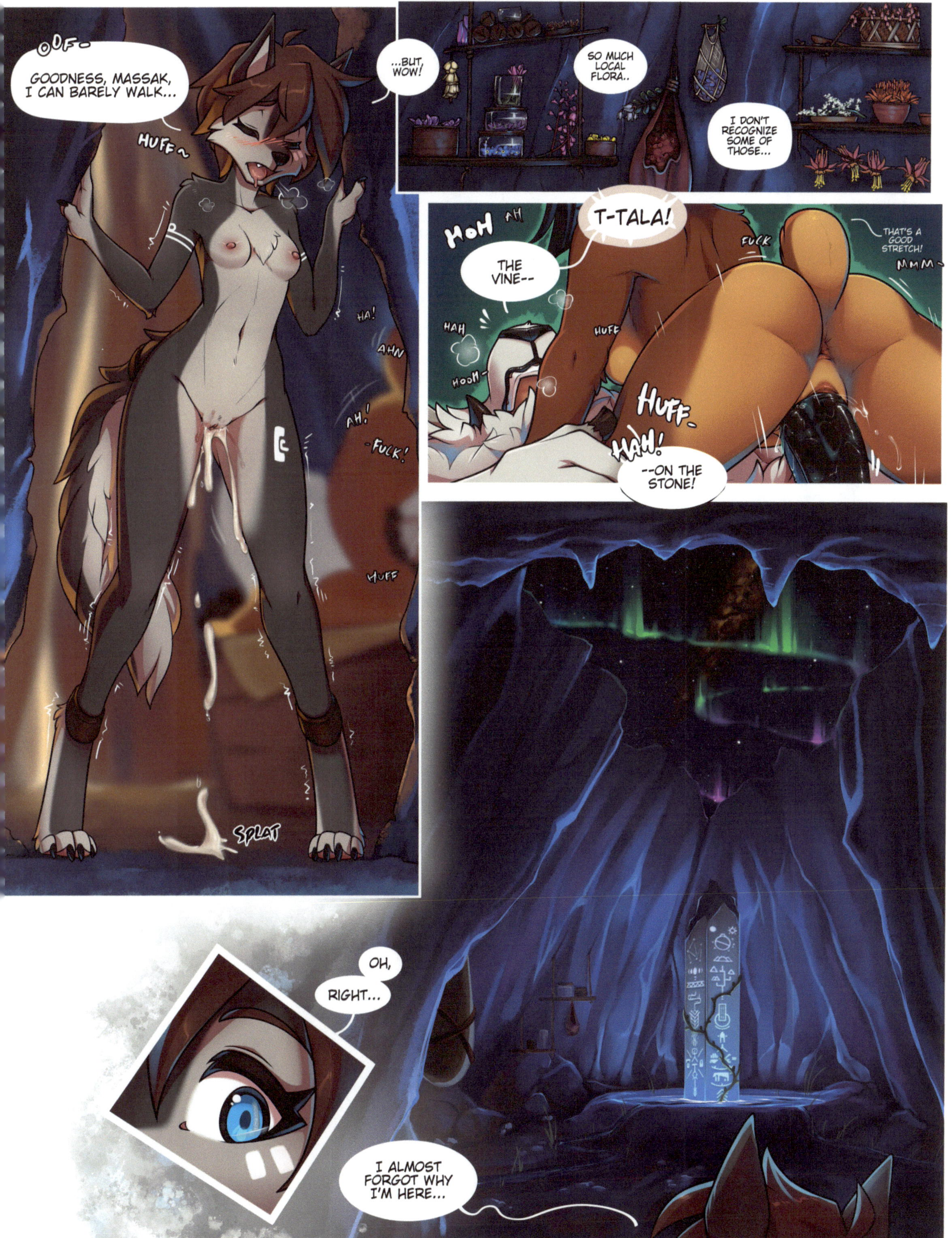
OOF-
GOODNESS, MASSAK, I CAN BARELY WALK...
HUFF~
...BUT, WOW!
SO MUCH LOCAL FLORA..
I DON'T RECOGNIZE SOME OF THOSE...
MOH
AH
HAH
HOOH-
T-TALA!
THE VINE--
FUCK
THAT'S A GOOD STRETCH!
MMM-
HUFF
HUFF-
HAH!
--ON THE STONE!
HA!
AHN
AH!
-FUCK!
HUFF
SPLAT
OH,
RIGHT...
I ALMOST FORGOT WHY I'M HERE...

'THE LONG CLIMB'. TO REACH THE SUMMIT SPRING AND CARRY ITS WATER BACK DOWN...

I THOUGHT THEY MEANT MELTED SNOW. NO ONE TOLD ME IT LOOKED LIKE →THIS←.

IT'S BEAUTIFUL, YET STRANGE.

TO THINK I ALREADY HAD SO MANY QUESTIONS. ABOUT BEING A WOLF, A LADY...NOW THIS?

OH, THE SEEDS MASSAK WAS TALKING ABOUT...

I...WISH I COULD STAY ON DENALI. WITH BAE'LI, MASSAK, TO MEET THE EAGLES AND LEARN ABOUT ALL OF THIS...

BUT NOW I'M JUST REMINDED OF MY CLIMB, AND GOING BACK TO KIGA.

SIGH~

...?

BWAH!
W-WHO ARE YOU?!
SPLASH
FORGIVE ME,
THIS IS THE FIRST TIME I HAVE BEEN ABLE TO VISIT A KINDRED SPIRIT OF OUR BLOOD IN PERSON. A RARE CONNECTION.
I AM FROM YOUR K'ELAAGE YOO.*
*=ANCESTORS
CALL ME AURORA.
ANCESTOR?!
GULP~
WHY DO YOU SOUND FEARFUL, 'YOUNG RIVER'?
I...EARLIER, THAT TRANCE I FELL UNDER...
AH,
IT IS TRUE, A FEW OF OUR WOLVEN SPIRITS-- THEY SEEK A HUNT.
BUT THEY DO NOT REPRESENT ALL OF US. YOU ARE LIKE ME.
YOU ARE FREE.
..FREE..?

YOUR BODY PROCEEDED WITH THE CLIMB, DESPITE YOUR DOUBTS.
YOUR SPIRIT BROKE FREE OF THE TRANCE, WHEN YOU THOUGHT YOU HAD HURT PREY.
AND YOUR HEART CHOSE TO ACT UPON ATTRACTION, DESPITE THE 'NATURAL ORDER'.
WELL, WHEN YOU PUT IT THAT WAY...
BUT THEY WERE -:YOUR:- DOING, YOUNG RIVER...
THEN WHY...DO I STILL FEEL SO ALONE?
TALA, WE ARE KINDRED SPIRITS--
I TOO, DID NOT HUNT, AND I TOO, ENJOYED THE INTIMACY OF BOTH PREDATOR AND PREY.
THAT BEING SAID...
WE ARE RARE EXCEPTIONS.
IN THIS WORLD, ATTRACTION BETWEEN PREDATOR AND PREY IS CLOUDED BY A VEIL.
FEW CAN SEE THROUGH IT; YOU, ME...YOUR BEAR FRIEND.
IN THE HEAVENS I FOUND MORE OF US. USING ALL OF OUR SPIRIT TOGETHER--
WE CREATED A SEED THAT HELPS DISSOLVE THAT VEIL.
HAA
AH -
HUFF-
HAAH
HAH
AHN
FUCK!
SPLT
PAP
PAP
THWP
WE HAD TO HOPE THAT OVER TIME, ITS USES WOULD BE FOUND.

THOSE SEEDS! ARE..YOURS?!
YES, TALA. DENYAAGHE*, OR DENYA. THEY ARE VERSATILE AND POTENT, WITH A WIDE RANGE OF EFFECTS.
*=PLANT/BEANS
IN ITS RAW FORM, CLOSE PROXIMITY CAN CAUSE DREAMS, HEIGHTENED SENSES, OR LIFTING SAID 'VEIL.'
I'VE FELT THAT!!
PRESSED INTO OIL, IT ALLOWS ALL SIZES OF BREEDING PARTNERS.
BOILED, AS THAT SHEEP HAS DONE, CREATES A STAMINA NECTAR ALSO CAPABLE OF BREEDING HYBRID OFFSPRING.
--THOUGH IT MAY TAKE TIME.
IT CAN WHAT!?!
HAH
AH
NGH..
HUFF-
AH
HAH
°OHH-
FF-UCK!!
PLIP
SPLT
GLP
R-REALLY?
YES, IF IT IS TRULY DESIRED.
PLOP!
THE ATTRACTION IS NOT FORCED-- IT ONLY ALLOWS IT, IF IT IS THERE, TO PASS THE VEIL.
SPLURT-

SO MY FEELINGS WERE REAL, BUT I WOULDN'T HAVE ACTED UPON IT UNLESS THE SEEDS WERE HERE...
HOW...CAN WE SHARE THIS?! THE FREEDOM TO CHOOSE ANY MATE-- THIS COULD HELP →EVERYONE←!
BUT...
"EAT MAGIC SEEDS! BREED WITH PREY!"
SOUNDS A LITTLE CRAZY.
ROP!
HAH..
AH..
ha-
SHLP
HOW BOUT... hff ...BIG BROWN BEAR BUTT?
SHAKE
PLP
HEHE, TALA...

'DENYA' IS, TRUE TO ITS NAME, A SEED.
PLANT IT.
AS IT GROWS, IT WILL EXPAND THE SAPIENT RANGE THAT SURROUNDS THE WORLD'S MOUNTAIN STONES.
THE AURA THAT LETS US THINK, SPEAK, AND STAND ON TWO FEET.
HOW MANY THINGS CAN THIS SEED DO?!
MANY! BUT... IT WILL NOT DRINK WATER.
OH..?
THIS SEED GROWS FROM MORTAL "SEED". A MIX OF WILLING PREDATOR AND PREY.
...OH.
NUDGE
NGH! SLAP!
HAA!
F-FUCK-
SLP
...AURORA... THAT'S LEWD.
HEHE. PERHAPS...
SPLT

SO...AM I...
PREGNANT?
NOT YET.
WE BELIEVE HYBRIDS WILL HELP WEAR DOWN THE VEIL.
AND WHILE THE SEED MAKES THEM POSSIBLE,
YOU'LL HAVE TO LIFT TAIL MORE THAN A FEW TIMES, SHOULD YOU WANT IT.
I'M SURE THIS SHEEP IS A "YES"...
HAVE YOU THOUGHT OF ANY BEARS IN THAT WAY?
BEAR DICK...?
Y..YES...
LET ME GUESS, IT'S A KIND BEAR?
YOU HAVE A GOOD HEART, TALA. YOUR ATTRACTION IS TO KINDNESS, NOT SPECIES, OR SIZE...
ꜰꜰ'AANO!*
YOUR CLIMB IS COMPLETE.
*=WELL DONE!
YOU'LL FIND THE WORDS. AND LOOK.
WAIT, WHAT?
I STILL DON'T KNOW WHAT TO TELL MY PACK!

WAIT, WHAT-?!
THANK YOU FOR BEING AS KIND AS I HOPED.
I AM SO VERY GLAD TO HAVE FOUND YOU,
BUT THIS IS YOUR JOURNEY TO FINISH.
WH-WHAT'S GOING ON?!
TELIDA HAVE ALWAYS GIVEN NEW MARKINGS TO THOSE WHO CLIMB.
THEY WILL HELP PROVE YOUR TALE.
YOU ARE NO LONGER A 'YOUNG RIVER', BUT A 'NORTHERN ARROW'.
FOLLOW YOUR HEART'S COMPASS.
THERE IS NO SHAME IN BEING NEK'EGHUN,*
*=WOLF
THERE ARE MORE KINDRED SPIRITS THAN JUST US...
...AND WE ARE ALWAYS WITH YOU.

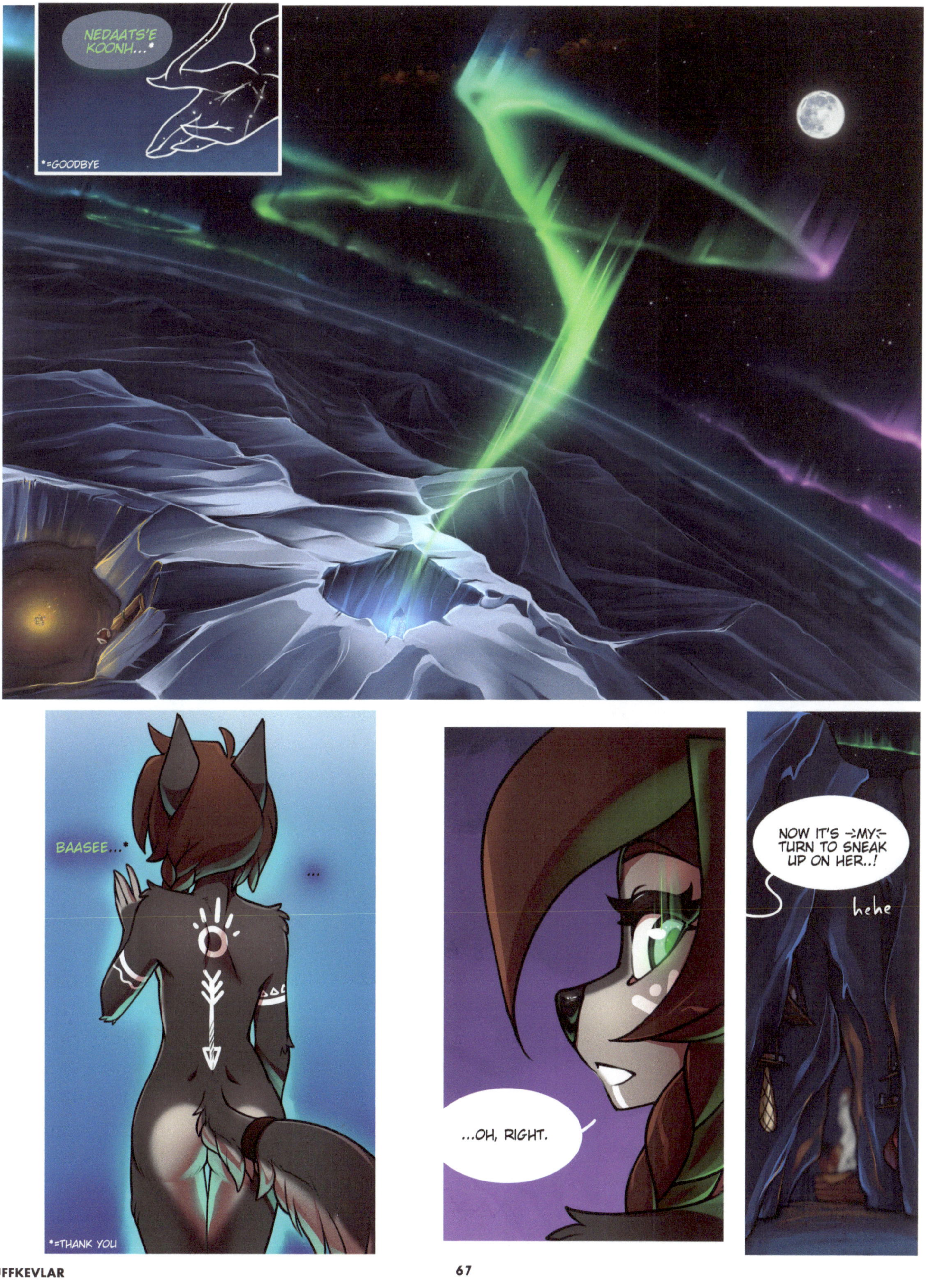

NEDAATS'E KOONH... *
*=GOODBYE

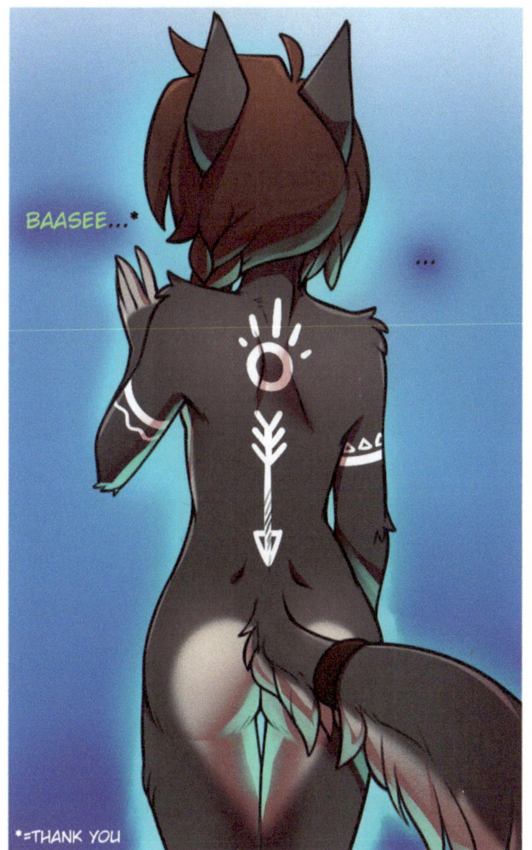

BAASEE...*
...
*=THANK YOU

...OH, RIGHT.

NOW IT'S →MY← TURN TO SNEAK UP ON HER..!
hehe

I MUST ADMIT, I WASN'T SURE YOU'D LET ME...HAVE AT YOU?
SPEAKING OF, WHERE'S TALA?
YOU HIDE THOSE SEEDS OR SOMETHING?!
HAH
HUFF
SQUISH
I COULD SAY THE SAME TO YOU, BIG GUY. THAT PRED/PREY LINE IS PRETTY THICK!
OH, I FOUND THEM ALRIGHT!
hehe
-AND I SEE YOU TWO GETTING ALONG QUITE NICELY!
TALA!
WHAT HAPPENED?! YOUR MARKINGS-- YOUR HAIR!
WELL--
HAIR?!
WHAT ABOUT YOUR FUCKING EYES?!

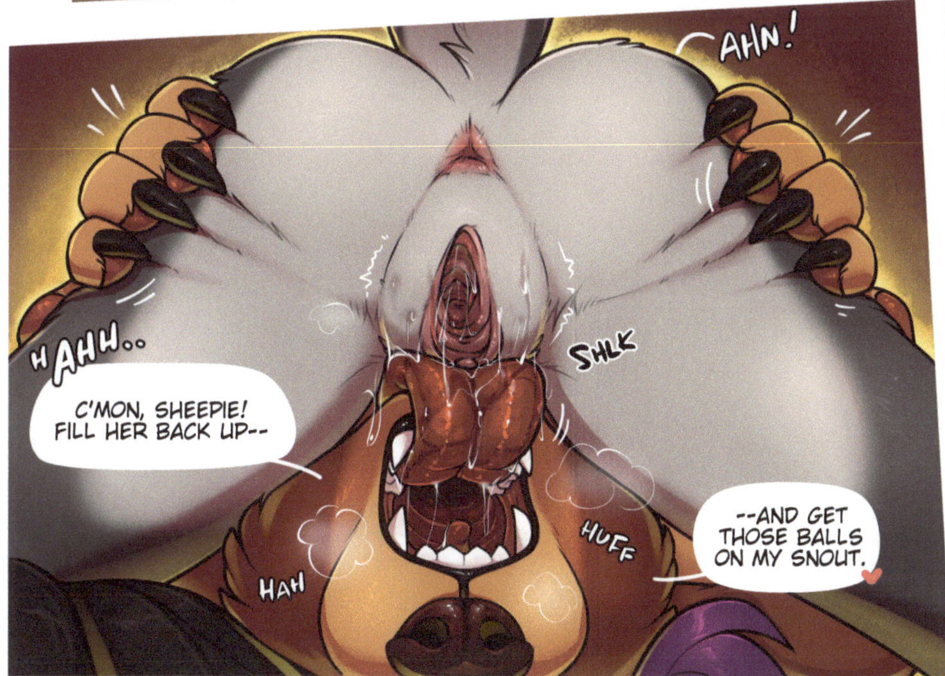
THEY'RE GREEN! AND--H-HEY, WHAT'RE YOU DOING..?
WELL... YOU'RE STARTING TO RUB OFF ON ME. SO I'D SAY--
IT'S ->MY<- TURN TO CLEAN ->YOU<-!
SHLPK~
SHLK
SLP
SHLK
O-OHHHH!
MM MN~
H-HA H..
AH..
LAP
SLP
LAP
LICK
SLRP
LAP
SLP
MMMN..
LAP
LAP
SLP
SHLK
ALRIGHT, LET ME PAY BACK YOUR PAYBACK.
GOSH, FORGOT HOW CUTE YOUR PUSSY IS.
THEY'RE SO...
NICE!
AHN!
H AHH..
SHLK
C'MON, SHEEPIE! FILL HER BACK UP--
--AND GET THOSE BALLS ON MY SNOUT.
HAH
HUFF

Y-YES, LADIES!
I ->HAVE<- TO BE DREAMING--
I MUST DOCUMENT THIS AS SOON AS I WAKE!

PREDATORS of Denali
YOU TWO ARE VERY HUNGRY PREDATORS, YOU KNOW THAT?
GUESS MY CURIOSITY ABOUT WHAT HAPPENED IN THERE WILL HAVE TO WAIT!
SO, THIS IS FOR YOU, TALA?
MHMM!
...WITH THESE 'ON YOUR SNOUT', MISS BAE'LI?
YESSS!
AND DON'T YOU WORRY SHEEPIE, I CAN TELL YOU,
I DID FIND OUT A THING OR TWO--
I'M SURE IT CAN WAIT, NOW LIFT THAT TAIL!
HEHEH, THINK I COULD FILL YOU UP ENOUGH TO GIVE YOU PUPS?
WELL, ACTUA-
AAH!
-SMAK-
-SLAP-
OOH-
-THWAK-
H-HA!
-SLAP-
F-FUCK--!
FLUFFKEVLAR
70

PREDATORS of Denali
M-MASSAK!
YOU'RE REALLY G-GONNA BREED ME IF YOU--
HAH!
AH!
HA-
HAH
HA-HHAH
HAH
HAH--HAH-
I CAN FILL YOU UP EVEN FURTHER NOW?!
GRIP
SQZ
SMK
SLAP
SMAK
THWAP
SHLK
HUFF
HUFF
SHLK
SLAP
BMP
GOOD STARS, WHAT A HEFTY BELLY BULGE..
I JUST WANNA--
SLP
SHLK
--MAKE HIM FEEL THIS TONGUE FROM OUTSIDE!
SSLP
HFF
HAH!
THESE LADIES...
AHh
FLUFFKEVLAR
71

-ARE GOING TO DRAIN ME!
HNN~
HAAAH--
HAA-
HFF
HAH
AH-WOOF!
WHUF
Y-YEAH...
B.. BREED ME!
SPLK-
PLP-
SPLT~
PLP-
TWITCH
THROB
PULSE
HA
SHLLIP!
AAAH...
MMMHH, FUCK.
NOW...
POP!
HAH
AAH~
MAMA BEAR WANTS HER HONEY. ♥
SLRK
NGH~HH...
GLP!
O-OH GOSH, M-MASSAK! HEHE, WELL SHE -÷DID÷- SAY SHE WAS HUNGRY...
HNH
Y-YOU LADIES COULD HAVE ME ALL NIGHT IF WE--
hehe
BAE'LI'S MOUTH IS FULL BUT I'M SURE SHE AGREES!
NGH-
I'M JUST SURPRISED YOU CAN KEEP GOING!
HH--NNH FFH...
HFF-
SHLP
SHLK
K-KEPT USING THE SEEDS..!
SLK
SLRP
HAH-
HUFF
SHLK-
MHH-HMN!

HAAH!
GLK!
HFF!
GLK
GULP.
GH-HH!
GULP!
GLP--
MHH!
SMAK!
MMMH..
AH
FF-FUCK--
HAH..
HA
HA..
HA
SLRP
HA
SUCK
WHUFF!
SLP
AH
NGH!
HFF!
HAH..
HA
AAAH!
SMAK
AH..
HUFF
SHLP
HFF
HNN-
SHLK
HAHH!
NH-

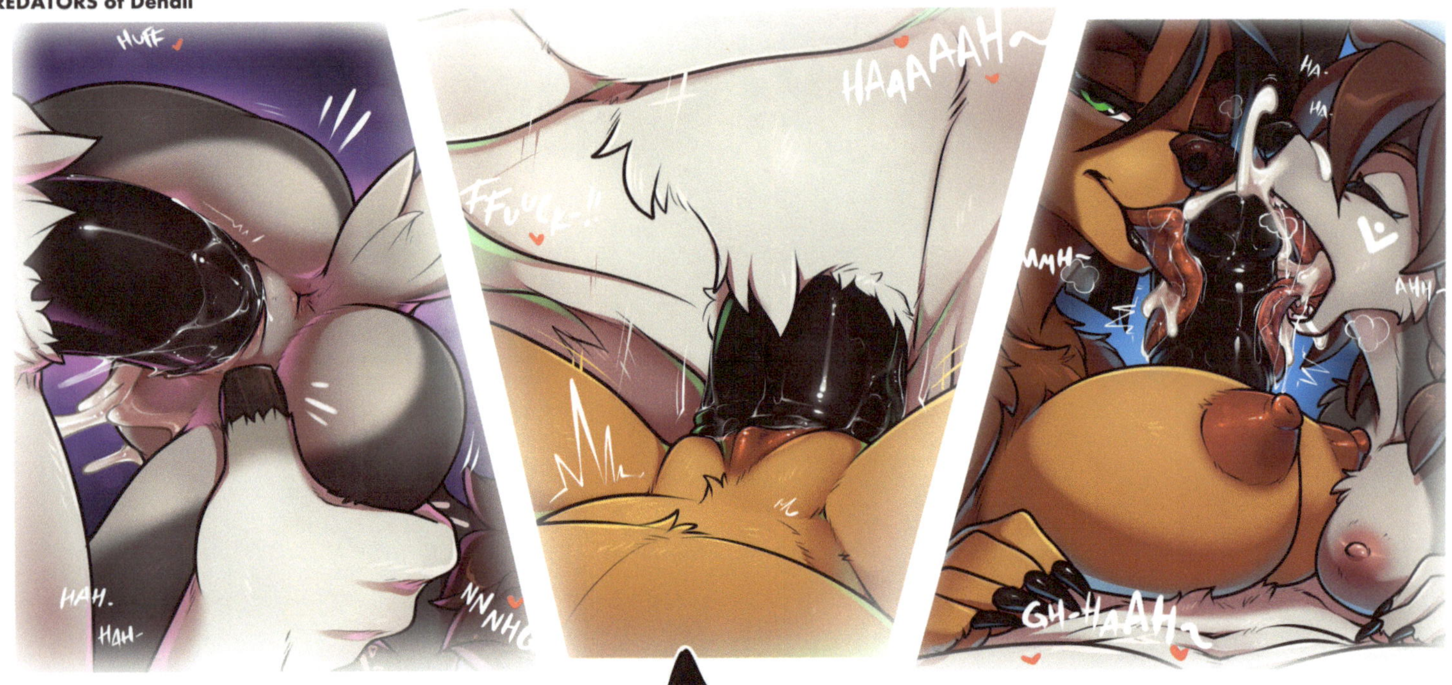
HUFF
HAAAAAH~
HA.
HA
FFUUK-!!
MMH~
AMH~
HAH.
HAH.
NNNHG
GH-HAAH~
AHH~
HAH..
HAAH..
HA...
AH..
WHUFF..
HUFF..
MMF..
HFF..
BA-A-A-AH..
HFF.
AHH..
HAH..
IT'S...ALMOST
MORNING...

HM...
TALA,
WHILE THIS WAS →EASILY← THE BEST 'WOLF CLIMB' I'VE TAGGED ALONG ON,
'YOUNG RIVER' MIGHT HAVE SAID 'YES', BUT I THINK 'NORTH ARROW' ME FEELS LIKE I CAN CHOOSE--
WHAT NOW? YOU JUST...GO BACK?
I JUST NEED TO HANDLE THE OUTCOMES OF THOSE CHOICES...

WOW.
THAT IS A GOOD WISDOM.
AND YOU LEARNED THAT JUST FROM HAVING SEX? HOW?! I DIDN'T LEARN ANYTHING!
HAHA, NO!
IT WAS EVERYTHING. EVERYONE. YOU, MASSAK, AURORA...
...WHO?
ER...THE AURORA!
THAT TRANCE...I THINK I'M TOO EASILY SHAPED BY OTHERS. I SHOULD BE MORE FORWARD WITH THAT →I← WANT.

AND THAT IS..?
ehe...
...THAT I STAY WITH YOU?
YEES!
Y-YEAH?
YOU KIDDING?! THAT'D BE GREAT!
FISHING, EXPLORING...
SHAKE
SHAKE

--WE COULD COME BACK HERE ANY TIME, TOO!
HMM- HMM~

I'VE...PACKED SOME SEEDS FOR YOU! DO COME BACK AND LET ME KNOW WHAT THE PREDATORS FIND..!
OH! THANK YOU MASSAK--
AND DON'T BE SILLY, OF COURSE WE WILL BE BACK!
AH, GOOD! I...REALLY ENJOYED THE COMPANY!
I DID TOO!!

IF YOU TWO DON'T HURRY IT UP WITH THE CUTE GOOD-BYES, THIS HUNKY RAM AURA IS GONNA MAKE MY CLOTHES DISAPPEAR.
AGAIN.

YOU KNOW, I HAVE A LOT OF RESEARCH ON PLANTS UP HERE,
WHY DON'T YOU COME BACK WITH TALA AND I'LL TEACH YOU WHAT I'VE FOUND?

OOOOOH?
HEY!
WHAT HAPPENED TO 'HURRY IT UP'?!
TUG
TUG

OH, AND BEFORE I FORGET--
hehe
H-HEY!
NOM

*=GOOD LUCK, FRIEND!
GGANAA'!*
WHO KNOWS, WE MIGHT RETURN WITH YOUR CUBS!
SEE YOU, FLUFFY BOY!

SO WITH OTHER TRIBES' HELP...

WE COULD QUELL THE DESIRE TO HUNT, EXPAND THE SAFE AREA AROUND THE MOUNTAIN STONES...
MAYBE MORE!
WELL, THEY MAKE A GREAT GREEN DYE! IF NOTHING ELSE, WE COULD SELL THAT.
BAE'LI...

...AND TO THINK MY LONG CLIMB WAS TO JUST BRING BACK SOME SYMBOLIC WATER.
I MEAN, TELLING THEM "I CLIMBED THE MOUNTAIN, ATE MAGIC SEEDS AND SAW SPIRITS" DOES SOUND A TAD CRAZY.
THAT'S WHAT I SAID! IT STILL FEELS LIKE A WEIRD DREAM...

SO HOW →WILL← YOU CONVINCE THE TELIDA PACK TO LET YOU STAY? AND TO TRY THESE SEEDS?
REALLY, THERE'S ONLY →ONE← WOLF I NEED TO CONVINCE...

--YOU LIE ABOUT YOUR CLIMB, SNEAKING OFF TO FIND SOMEONE WHO KNOWS OUR PACK'S MARKINGS TO DECIEVE ME,
K-KIGA--
AND YOU WANT TO LEAVE THE PACK?! 'NORTHERN ARROW'?!
KIGA!
BORK
SNARL
YOU--
YOU WILL HEAR ME!!
LISTEN! YOU WANT TO SAVE OUR ROLE AS PROTECTORS?
--THEN IT HAS TO BE A →WOLF← TO HELP STOP THIS!
I REALIZED WHY ONE AS WEAK AND SMALL AS ME IS NEK'EGHUN*.
*=WOLF
I'M NON-THREATENING. PREY CAN TRUST ME.
YOU SAID IT YOURSELF-- WE EITHER WORK TOGETHER, OR FALL TO HUNTING THEM!
WE'LL BE NO DIFFERENT THAN THE FERALS WE GUARD AGAINST. TO THEM, WE'LL ALL JUST BE
PREDATORS.
...
SHE...HAS A POINT!
heheh..
A WOLVEN DIPLOMAT WOULD BE WELL-RECIEVED OVER A THIRD-PARTY...
SHE MAY STAY WITH BAE'LI!

THE PACK OUTSIDE IS READY TO RETURN, KIGA.
...FINE.
I'M TRUSTING YOU, TALA. DO NOT LET TELIDA DOWN.
SHE'LL BE FINE. THE URSA TRIBE WILL SEE YOU OFF NOW, 'GRUMPY-BIG-SNOOT.'
WH...WHAT DID YOU CALL ME..?
TUG
TUG

AHA! WONDERFUL! WE MUST PREPARE A CELEBRATION FOR OUR NEWEST TRIBE MEMBER!
IT WORKED...
G'HAAN, LET US PREPARE TOMORROW FOR A WELCOMING!

TOMORROW?
GOT YOUR OWN WELCOME PLANS FOR ME TONIGHT?
DOES BIG 'DADDY BEAR' WANT SOME 'WOLF HONEY'?
..HH--
HEHH?!
AH..AH-HAH! A JOKE..!
P-PLEASE, JUST CALL ME 'ASKA'!!
TAP
TAP

SORRY,
IT JUST FEELS GOOD TO BE FREE...TO SAY, GO, AND DO ANYTHING...
I'M GOING TO CATCH BAE'LI! TEASE YOU LATER!
YOU'LL...WAIT, WHAT?!?
...YOU--
BUT WASN'T SHE SHY BEFORE?
THAT'S NOT POSSIBLE.
DID SHE REALLY SAY THA--
IS THAT EVEN THE SAME WOLF?
CAN'T BE SERIOUS ABOUT THAT, RIGHT?
IT'S BEEN A WHILE
BUT I'D CRUSH HER..!
HAH..AHAH... OH DEAR.

GOSH, I HAVEN'T FELT LIKE THIS IN...EVER! WHERE DO I EVEN BEGIN..?
SEEDS, STONE, TRIBES...IT'S A LONG TO-DO LIST, BUT I THINK I GOT THIS.
IT'S STRANGE TO NOT FEEL INTIMIDATED.
AURORA WAS RIGHT. BAE'LI TOO. SPEAKING OF WHOM...
...WHERE IS SHE?
LET ME GUESS...
IS THIS TO MAKE ME "FORGET ABOUT TALA"?
MH-HMM!
ahn-
hah
ha
huff
SLK-
SHLP
SLRP
WELL, IT'S WORKING...
huff..
wuff...
SHLK-
MH4~
SSSHLK!
Mmm-
SHLP
END.

THANK YOU FOR READING!

Thank you to all of you who have supported me on Patreon, sub-scribestar, Etsy, and more, that helped make this comic possible! Thank you to my friends and fellow artists for feedback, critique, and to my wife Rei, who provided me with all that and then some, as I worked to make the best comic I could.

Predators of Denali has given me lots of practice, ideas, and techniques to use, or not use, in future work and endeavours. I've learned a lot about story and comics over the course of these 6 years. I will definitely revisit these characters-- maybe even in some sequel side-comics in the future!

...As long as they don't take another 6 years.

www.ingramcontent.com/pod-product-compliance
Lightning Source LLC
Chambersburg PA
CBHW040825050726
47507CB00021B/136